W9-BCN-843

ROSIE'S WALK

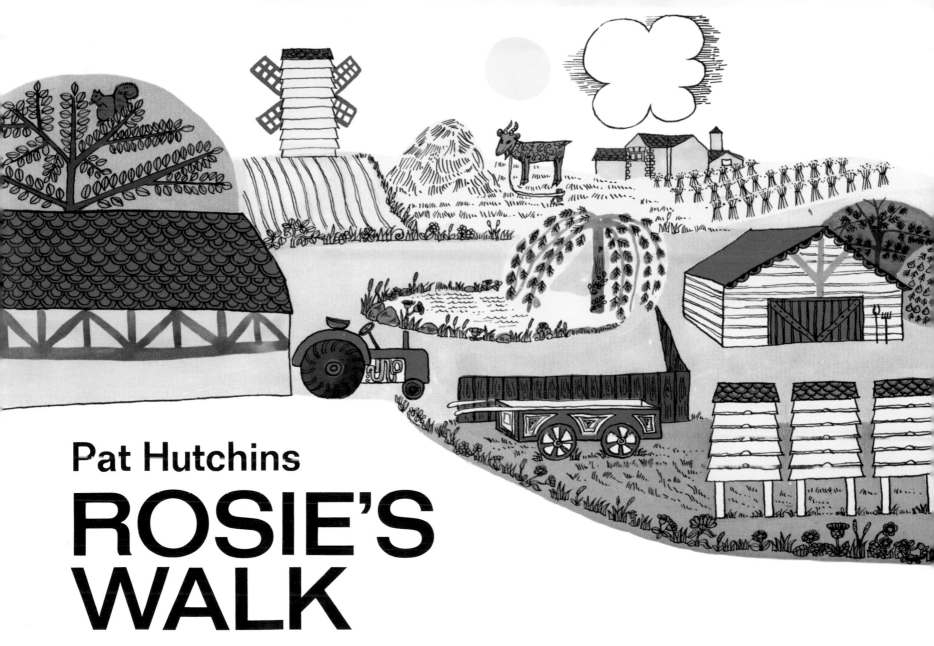

Pat Hutchins
ROSIE'S WALK

ALADDIN PAPERBACKS

Aladdin Paperbacks
An imprint of Simon & Schuster
Children's Publishing Division
1230 Avenue of the Americas
New York, NY 10020

First Aladdin Paperbacks Edition, 1986

Rosie's Walk is published in a hardcover edition by
Simon & Schuster Children's Publishing Division.

Manufactured in China

56 58 60 59 57

Library of Congress catalog card number: 68-12090

ISBN 978-0-02-043750-5
0415 SCP

For
Wendy
and
Stephen

Rosie the hen went for a walk

across the yard

around

the

pond

over the haystack

past the mill

through the fence

under the beehives

and
got back
in time
for dinner.